Some Tales from Romney Marsh

For the young and not-so-young!

Written by Nick Russell

Illustrated by Maikki Ranger

All Rights reserved

No part of this publication may be reproduced, stored in a retrieval system, or transmitted in any form or by any means without the prior permission in writing of the publisher, nor be otherwise circulated in any form of binding or cover other than that in which it is published and without a similar condition including this condition being imposed on the subsequent purchaser.
The moral right of the author has been asserted.

First published in the UK by Nick Russell 2022

Printed and bound in the UK by Adam's of Rye

Contents

Introduction	5
Stories:	
The Most Unusual and Exotic Bird!	7
The Big Fire	14
The Monster from the Deep	24
The Big Rave	34
The Beach Rescue	43
Snowed up and Iced in	50
Beach Landings	61
Tess and Ivan's Wedding	71

Thanks

With thanks to my niece Maikki for all her hard work and creativity in producing the illustrations which have helped to bring the stories and characters to life!

Thank you to Annie Chown for allowing us to use her photographs of Hastings fishermen as inspiration for some of the illustrations.

Thanks to Romney Marsh author, Emma Batten, for her support and helping me bring my stories and characters to life. Without Emma's guidance, mentoring and encouragement this fledgling author might never have written these stories.

Introduction

The Romney Marsh is a wondrous thing,
The land between two seas.
From Rye in in the west to Hythe in the east
It is rich in its diversity (eee).

From its folk to its shores,
Its lore and its mores
Are something you all should see!

These stories are fictitious but based in fact, born of my long experience growing up, living, working and, above all, enjoying living on or around the Romney Marsh for more than 50 years. All characters are fictional.

While some of the tales are light-hearted, others reflect a message about the importance of working as a community and supporting others In these changing and uncertain times. The stories are intended for the young and not-so-young, and it is hoped they will appeal to adults and visitors. From a tattoo artist to a farmhand, from countryside to coast, follow my characters in this series of short stories for the young and young-at-heart…

Nick Russell 2022

That Most Unusual and Exotic Bird!

Turdly Turd was quite a bird
Feathers all akimbo
Cruising around the chimney pots
While the world was in limbo

No one knew where the strange flapping creature came from. But suddenly she was there living amongst them, and everyone was talking about her.

There were all sorts of birds who visited Dungeness. For some of them it was the first time their spindly legs had landed on the ground for several days or weeks. They flew from many areas of the world before spending their holidays amongst the stones, lakes and reed beds.

Nobody had seen a bird like this before. There were huge black cormorants with great craggy wings. There were dainty white avocets, and tiny reed warblers clinging to thin stems. Ducks came in their swarms and geese honked as they flew overhead. This new bird was a mystery though.

"Never spotted one like it before."

"Quick – the camera."

"Over there – can you see?"

The birdwatchers swarmed to Dungeness. They scrambled over the stony ground and spent hours in the hides, all hoping to see this oddity.

What did she look like – this bird, so different to any seen before? She was big. Bigger than big – quite gigantic. At first the birdwatchers said her wings were black, but then they saw different colours shimmering on the tips - sometimes red, sometimes orange or yellow. The birders scribbled pictures of this newcomer. They drew long legs, and coloured them orange, a curved neck and huge round eyes. There were tufts of feathers on top of her head, and the very ends of them looked like they had been dipped in paint pots of red, orange and yellow. On her face they coloured a large beak and a splat of yellow around it.

"She must come from foreign parts," the birdwatchers agreed.

After a couple of weeks, people stopped dashing madly to see this bird. It seemed she was here to stay. They also understood that they didn't need to sneak around or hide away to catch a glimpse of the crazy creature. The birders – and everyone else – realised that the new bird was a big show-off! There seemed to be nothing she liked better than spinning in the sky and performing loop-the-loops. When she sat on the top of a tree or on the roof of one of the wooden homes by the sea, she would stretch her neck out and flap her huge wings.

The local chippy on the beach was a favourite spot for people to gather. They began to offer fishy treats to the bird, and it soon got to love a titbit of battered cod.

*

"I've been asked to design a flag!" Tess told her friends. "Have you heard about this new bird at Dungeness?" Tess was an amazing artist. She usually created tattoos

"I've been asked to design a flag!" Tess told her friends. "Have you heard about this new bird at Dungeness?"

on her customers' bodies, as well as her own. Arms, legs... and other places hidden beneath clothes! Her arty ways didn't stop on her skin – Tess's hair changed colour every week. Today it was mostly blonde with dark ends twisted into a plait.

Fred was a farmhand at Reed Farm, and Ed lived on the farm with his sister and parents. He was only twelve but managed to persuade Fred to let him tag along sometimes. They were good friends of Tess, and her biker boyfriend, Ivan. Now the four of them were sitting on the green at Littlestone with ice creams.

"I've heard of it and seen it!" Ed replied. "It was out at the farm yesterday, flying around like a crazy thing. But what's it got to do with a flag?"

"It's the chippy," Tess explained. "They want her on a flag. A bit like a mascot. I said I would go over there sometime."

"Well, if there are fish and chips on offer..." Fred grinned.

"Let's go!" Ed finished. He crammed the last of his ice cream into his mouth.

They raced to Ivan's car – a real old banger with flames painted down the sides. Within ten minutes, the team were parking up at Dungeness. "It's crowded here today," Ivan observed, as they found a wooden table outside the fish and chip shop.

"It's the bird!" Aeleen called out, passing by with plates of fish and chips. "It's got so busy in the last couple of weeks. Look! There she goes now." Aeleen served a couple sitting at a nearby table, then continued. "It's like she has a daily patrol. They say she's been seen as far away as Dymchurch and Camber."

"People are saying that she's giving an alert if there's danger or trouble," Ivan told Ed and Fred, who were gazing up as the unusual bird stopped mid-flight and performed a series of twirls. "It seems hard to believe, but it's happened a few times."

"Eyes in the sky!" Ed suggested.

"Yes!" Aeleen agreed. "There's a family from Greatstone who say the bird saved their child's life when he started drifting out to sea on an inflatable swan! She flew off and let the coastguard know!"

As they chatted, more locals walked over. It seemed that everyone had something to say about the bird.

"She's got her own language!"

"A flap of her wing, or a weird squawk, and the

coastguard or the helicopter crew know what she's trying to say."

"We need a name for her…"

"Something crazy… barmy?"

"There's an odd whiff about her!"

"Turdly Turd – The Exotic Bird!"

The name stuck and so Turdly settled down to life on Romney Marsh, becoming part of the ebb and flow of the birds who lived or visited the area. As the weeks and months passed, it seemed as if she formed a special attachment to the four friends, and not a day went by without one of them spotting her. The 'kingdom between two seas' was a special place to live and Turdly seemed to agree.

Author's note: The reason why I began writing these stories in the first place was because I dreamed up the characters of Turdly Turd, Ed (originally called Willy), Fred (originally Dick) plus Ivan and Tess "out of the blue, in the wee small hours", so felt compelled to write something! Very different from my main interest which is poetry.

The Fire

Turdly smelt the burning
Then she spied the scene
Saw the smoke
Then alerted the folk (at the farm)

It was the kind of summer where the sun beat down on Romney Marsh, day after day, week after week. It was a summer everyone would remember for years to come and say, "Do you remember that year when it didn't rain for months?" The crops had turned to a golden brown and the tramlines, used by the tractors to find their way about the swathes of nodding barley, had huge cracks opened up in them. The barley and wheat were tinder dry, and the oilseed rape – famed for its bright yellow flowers in the spring – was nothing but acres of blackened, gnarled seedheads.

You can imagine the hordes of visitors who travelled down the motorways and along the roads, looking forward to a day on the sandy beaches of Romney Marsh. Mostly, they suffered the traffic queues and enjoyed their day at Camber, Dymchurch or Greatstone. Sometimes they decided to explore the lesser-known country lanes of Romney Marsh and set up their picnic or barbecue at the edge of a field.

Mostly the visitors were careful, but with the ground so dry all it takes is one match, one spark, one ember and then wumf, next thing you have a wildfire or a crop fire on your hands…

As always, when he was at home on the farm, Ed was wearing tatty shorts and a t-shirt streaked in muck, oil and grease. His hair was still in whatever 'bed-head' crazy style he had woken up with. In contrast, his elder sister, Maggie, and her best friend, Lizzy, had spent half an hour fussing over their hair and….

"What's that blue stuff on your eyes?" Ed asked in wonder and disgust.

"Mind your own business," Maggie laughed. "You'll never get a girlfriend if you can't brush your hair."

"I wasn't looking for one." Ed shrugged. "I'm only twelve!" He refused to let the girls wind him up. That way he always had the better of them. What did they think they were doing hanging out on the farm with their faces painted like that? He grinned, wondering what his parents would have to say when they saw the girls. They might act all grown-up, but they were only a year older than him!

The three of them were sitting on the old wall at the

front of the even older farmhouse, eating toast and jam. They held it in their hands and licked sticky fingers as they ate.

"Did you make me any?" Fred called as he walked by pushing a barrow full of chicken muck.

"No!" the trio replied.

"No worries," Fred, the farmhand, replied. "Now, you know we've got to watch out for fires today. Lots of trippers out and it only takes one spark…"

"And it will spread like wildfire," Ed finished. Whereas most boys of his age were attached to their phones or a computer screen, he loved to be out in the fresh air and was wise to the ways of the countryside.

"Talking of wild." Fred looked at the sky. "There's that crazy bird! We'll have the place crawling with twitchers if she decides to keep coming over to Reed Farm."

They paused for a moment, watching the unique mass of scraggy black feathers, huge glossy eyes and long legs, swooping and whooping above the row of bent willow trees. No bird expert had been able to say where Turdly came from. Despite her curious selection of squawks and chirps, coupled with a frantic flapping of wings and peculiar little nods of her head, the bird was unable to tell them. However, everyone living on Reed

Farm agreed that it was fun having the exotic bird flying about in the skies above them or roosting in the willow trees at night.

"She must be a metre from wing to wing," Ed remarked.

"He's learned his measurements!" Maggie laughed.

Lizzy sniggered and Ed ignored them. There was work to be done – no time to be lingering over breakfast or watching the unusual bird. No time to be hanging around with annoying girls. "Are we still going to check the moisture in the crops?" he asked.

"We are!" Fred replied. "The Gaffer thinks we'll be ready to start on the fields by noon. He's checking over the combine harvester. Race you to the quads!"

"Hey! Turdly!" Ed called upwards, as he followed on Fred's heels. "Look out for fires. We could do with a pair of eyes in the sky!"

As if the bird understood his words, she seemed to pirouette in the blue and let out a long, low screech.

By noon, the sun was at its highest point in the sky and there was not a cloud to be seen. The great monstrous beast of a harvester was beginning its lumbering journey across the fields of barley. The tractors – Fred driving one, and Ed's dad, who they called Gaffer, on the other

– lined up to collect the grain as it spewed out from the combine's chute and into trailers. Ed hung onto the back of Fred's seat to enjoy the ride as they trundled to and fro. Back in the farmyard, grain was deposited in barns whose metal walls shimmered in the heat.

With their hair no longer slickly styled, and eye make-up a mucky mess, Maggie and Lizzy loaded a box of drinks and doorstop sandwiches onto a quad bike. Their plans to catch the bus to Ashford were scuppered the moment it was announced that the barley was dry enough to harvest. Everyone out on the fields needed feeding, and the girls would be expected to help.

High in the sky – riding on the breeze – Turdly cruised about. She watched the harvesting and the girls on the quad bike. In the vegetable garden near the house, Mrs Gaffer, Mum to Maggie and Ed, could be spotted gathering runner beans from tall poles. By the Military Canal, in the furthest field from the farm buildings, a piece of something shone and glinted. Turdly decided to swoop closer and investigate. All her birdy instincts told her this could lead to trouble.

The sun reflected on the metal of a discarded barbecue. Long, dry grass began to smoulder against it, and a tiny flame grew. Hovering not far from the ground, Turdly somersaulted, her tiny heart racing. As the exotic bird hung in the sky, a ribbon of flames shot along the edge of the field.

Turdly tore off as fast as her wings could carry her. She knew where The Gaffer and Fred were working in the barley field and was determined to alert them.

Fire! Fire! Turdly warned, placing her wings in a point for as long as she could hold the position, before swooping around and repeating the gesture. Over there! Over there by the canal! The bird squawked and nodded towards the west.

"Something's wrong!" Fred called out, waving his arms to alert Gaffer.

"Over there! Fire!" Ed pointed to the narrow plume of smoke.

Within minutes the combine and one tractor had been abandoned as they piled onto quad bikes and returned

to the farmyard with the smaller tractor. Mrs Gaffer was calling the fire brigade while the others were loading the bashed-up old Landrover with fire beaters. Meanwhile, the Gaffer was attaching a plough to the tractor.

The wail of fire engines could be heard by the time everyone had reached the far field. The Gaffer took no notice of them but stood for a moment studying the wind direction. "Take it across there," he ordered Fred.

Fred knew exactly what his boss meant. Within minutes, the tractor was being put to work. It destroyed lines of ripe wheat to create a firebreak. "We've got to lose this to save the rest," Fred muttered to himself. As he worked, he could see Ed, Maggie and Lizzy approaching the fire and using beaters to destroy any stray embers. Others joined them – local people coming from nearby fields. At a time like this the neighbouring farms would pull together to help each other.

Eventually, the wails of the sirens came closer, and two fire trucks lumbered across rutted tracks. The firemen placed wide pipes into the nearby canal, and the water was pumped until it gushed onto the flaming crops.

The Gaffer, his family and workers were lucky that day. The fire only reached the edge of the wheat field. The damage could have been a lot worse.

Maggie and Lizzie - their hair no longer slickly styled, and eye make-up a mucky mess!

In the evening, everyone gathered for a ploughman's supper. They sat on garden chairs or sprawled on picnic rugs. The family from the farm took turns to tell the strange story of the quirky bird who warned them about the fire. It was becoming dark, but they were all certain that Turdly was perched nearby in the branches of an oak tree. Maybe, just maybe, she was listening in.

"Turdly is a hero," Fred declared. "Doesn't seem right that she's got no proper home, and no one knows where she came from."

"You're right," said Ed. "How about we build her a shelter on the barn roof, so she can keep an eye on things. We'll make a good team here on the farm, and I've got a feeling wherever there is trouble – here in the countryside or over by the coast – Turdly will spot it."

"What do you think of that?" Maggie called up to the sky. "Your own house on the roof!"

From the darkness of the oak tree, there came a long shrill birdcall. Everyone laughed and began to tuck into their ice cream.

Author's note: When I was a student, I used to work on farms in the summer doing a variety of jobs. I remember helping fight several fires during this time.

The Monster from the Deep

On day two after the Big Storm
Turdly was in motion again
And noticed some commotion
On the beach near the power station.
Something mighty fishy going on!!!

It was mopping up time! There had been a great storm with the tide flowing higher than ever, and rain pouring from the sky. Seawater had flowed over the shingle banks at Greatstone, and ditches in the countryside had burst their banks – water flowed into homes and onto the roads.

Under the watchful eye of the emergency services, a

group of volunteers in high-viz jackets were on the scene. In small teams they were checking on vulnerable residents living along the coast road and making sure they were safe and dry.

"No one wants to be paddling about in their own home," Ivan commented, as he and Tess left an elderly couple. They had just given them the details of a hotel in New Romney which was offering rooms to those in need.

Tess gave him a hug. "You're a lovely bloke!"

Some people kept their distance from Tess and Ivan. Just because she was a tattoo artist with hair that changed colour every week, and he had a ponytail hanging down the back of his leather biker jacket, it didn't mean they weren't decent people. They were the first to help out in the community when needed, and the first to join in with any fun to be had!

"Over here!" Fred called out. He and Ed were juggling paper cups of coffee and hot chocolate they had bought from a pop-up tent on the roadside. Maggie had a bag of warm doughnuts.

The friends flopped on the edge of the shingle bank overlooking the sea. The tide was midway up the sands, rolling in with none of the fury it had shown yesterday. They had been helping since early morning and deserved a break. Maggie handed out doughnuts, and they sat in silence for a moment, munching and licking sugary lips.

"There she goes," Tess said, nodding up to the sky. Turdly swooped past at a leisurely pace. They watched her glide past the fish and chip café near the beach and towards the lifeboat station. From their spot on the beach, the four friends could see the bright orange lifeboat resting on the bank outside its shed.

It seemed as if Turdly did an emergency stop up there in the sky. Her head and neck jerked upwards, and a curious squeal could be heard. Then rather than continue her path along the coast, the quirky bird did a loop-the-loop and sped towards the team on the beach. Once above them she squawked and nodded her head towards Dungeness.

"Looks like she wants us to follow," Ed spoke as he pulled himself up. "Come on."

They trudged along the shingle – it being almost impossible to run on the stones – and towards a group of fishermen. There were three of them telling stories of past adventures and making a drama out of all the small details. The friends had seen this many times before, but it always made them smile. This time the tales were being told to a young coastguard, a couple of dog walkers and a group of litter pickers. If they were lucky, these fishermen, who had lived at Dungeness all their lives, and their parents and grandparents before them, would earn a few pounds for entertaining the passers-by.

Crabbie was holding everyone's attention. "That was one of the worst storms I have seen in more than forty years on this beach. We're lucky that the boats haven't had much damage apart from a few knocks. I could tell you some tales about when we weren't so lucky…"

Pongo didn't want to miss out on his share of the telling. He butted in with his own memories. "The worst storm of all was in 1988. Now, that was a real terror – never seen another like it. I remember I was on the Saucy Sal in them days…"

"88!" Crabbie scoffed. "It was nothing but a ripple in a bathtub! You didn't even get your hair washed from the waves coming over. If you had, then your Annie would have been pleased!"

Pongo scowled. Determined to keep the attention on himself, he continued, "Anyway, it was never our boats that came off the worst. We know to watch the sea and the clouds, and we know when to head home. It's those

boats passing by that needed to watch out in the old days." He paused for dramatic effect. "Those Nessers used to forget about lighting the fire in the old lighthouse and if a ship happened to wash up on the stones, then they didn't think to help those poor sailors. Oh no! They would take what they could. Even the boats were useful. Made of wood, they were, and wood is handy for making things, isn't it? The old Pilot pub – now that was made from ship's timbers."

Ed turned to look back along the coast to the Pilot, a place known to be full of history and popular with visitors. "It's made from a boat?" he asked in disbelief.

"Why not?" Pongo asked. "Boats are made from good strong wood - nothing better!"

There was no chance for Ed to respond. Pasqual, squatting on an upturned crate with his friends, took a chance to entertain the small crowd. "There's a lot of strange things down there," he said, nodding towards the grey-green sea. "Some say it's because of the power stations. Some say it's the ghosts of dead fishermen. There's strange beasts about though…"

Everyone turned to look at the sea, expecting some kind of monster to rear up from the depths. A light mist was rolling in and the smell of salt and seaweed was rich in the air. The dogs were sniffing at an object washed up on the high tide mark. It made a peaceful scene and the idea of monsters lurking off the shore was hardly believable. Reluctantly, their owners left the fishermen and their tall tales to check everything was OK with their four-legged friends. Ed and Maggie followed. They had heard these stories time and time again. In the sky, Turdly hovered and looked down on the ragged line of seaweed, shells and driftwood.

"Look at this!" one of the dog owners said as the kids approached. He fastened a lead onto the dog's collar and tried to pull him off. "Never seen anything like it, have you…?"

Ed frowned as he stepped closer. The fish must have been eight feet in length, its body lean and lanky with metallic, bright green scales. Along the twisted back there was a row of spikes leading up to the head – NO! – heads! Somehow the beast had three of them, each one with a mouth full of pointed teeth.

"Come away, kid!"

Ed shuffled nearer. Part of him wanted to look at every detail of this monster - at its yellow eyes and the fronds at the end of its tail - but then the awful smell hit Ed's nostrils. He turned away and breathed deeply,

Heads! Somehow the beast had three of them, each one with a mouth full of pointed teeth!

thinking he was going to be sick. Glancing at Maggie, he saw that she had gone pale and had also backed off.

The next moment, Fred was with them, his hands on their shoulders. "Come away. They're calling the coastguard. This needs looking into properly." The friends moved but gathered nearby, watching while the area was fenced off with some the fishermen's crates.

"They'll be telling the Environment Agency about this, and then everyone will want to listen to my tales!" Pasqual was saying to anyone who would listen. "There will be experts here in no time. This is a weird beast, and I'm not surprised it's been washed up here."

"It was bound to happen," Crabbie agreed. "There's been changes since the nuclear power station was built. All the fishermen said the waters changed. My dad and uncle used to talk about it."

"There's been some strange fish caught in nets over the years," Pongo agreed. "But none as strange as this."

"They like to keep it quiet," Crabbie shot dark looks towards the coastguard. "But there's plenty of tales recounted around the fire at the Pilot or Britannia on stormy winter nights!"

The fishermen fell quiet as the coastguard walked over. "The experts are on their way," he reported. "This…

this… whatever it is… will be taken away to a laboratory somewhere for a close examination. In the meantime, the area is out of bounds. Understood?"

"Of course," Fred answered for them all. "There's more work to be done on clearing up after the storm. We need to move on." He turned away and began to climb the shingle bank at the top of the beach. Ed, Maggie, Tess and Ivan followed.

"How about some fish and chips before we get back to work?" Ivan asked as they approached the Chippy on the Beach.

Ed thought of the monster fish on the beach and his face turned an odd shade of green. "Depends what type of fish!" he replied, as they all turned towards the pub. "I think it might be a burger for me!"

"Same here!" Maggie said. For once, the brother and sister agreed!

Author's Note: Back in the 1960s, I used to go deep sea fishing out of Rye Harbour with my brother and friends. The wonderful skipper was the epitome of the salty old seadog and used to regale us with stories of 'strange fish that lurked in the depths of Rye Bay close to the new Dungeness Power Station'. He reckoned that the warm waters generated by the Power Station attracted all sorts of strange fish and even made some of them mutate into monster-like creatures. Some of the local fishermen had apparently caught weird creatures with two heads, like two-headed congers... Of course, this might be fishermen's tales, but there is no smoke without fire…

The Big Rave

Turdly sounded the alarm
Disturbing the weekend pints
Crowds gathering on Greatstone beach
Covid rules ignored
People could be harmed …
Ivan sounded the charge
And the gang sped down the beach
To help the police…

It was a hot August Saturday lunchtime. The beach was crowded. Lots of visitors! Covid restrictions had been eased, and people wanted to have fun. However, the rules were to stay in small groups, socially distance and NO big gatherings or beach parties. The local hospitals were still full of people who were very sick from the virus. The government used the words BIG SURGE – this would mean the coronavirus was getting out of control. Everyone hoped that would not happen.

Ed, Maggie and Lizzy had caught the bus to the coast and were walking along the seafront road towards Dungeness and the Chippy on the Beach. With the girls wearing coloured ribbons threaded through their hair and sequinned t-shirts, Ed was feeling a bit awkward about hanging out with them and hoped to meet one of his mates. But his mum had been generous with their pocket money as all three had been working hard on the farm. To go out for fish and chips was a real treat!

When he spotted Ivan's car, Ed had a feeling that Fred would be nearby. The farmworker might be a few years older, but he treated Ed like he was a friend, not a kid.

"There's Tess!" Maggie pointed towards the queue at the hatch before screeching, "Teeeeeessssss!!"

Ed had a feeling that Maggie and Lizzy secretly admired Tess's bold style and that was why they had twisted ribbons through their hair. They wouldn't be allowed to dye their long hair, but this was a start… He watched Maggie bound over, closely followed by Lizzy.

The girls ordered the food, while Ed scanned around for Fred and Ivan, then joined them on a long bench. Soon all six were making a cheerful crowd with lots of laughter and the mouth-watering smell of fried food.

Turdly was relaxing on the pub's roof. She could stay close to her friends and keep an eye on the coast.

"There she goes…" Maggie remarked, as the exotic bird took off. "She's taking flight towards Dymchurch."

"Bound to be trouble on a busy day like this," Fred commented.

Ivan replied, "I've been listening to the news and there are rumours a lot of people are going to descend on Greatstone beach this weekend for a covid rave! They reckon that it's a bit sleepy here, and a party will liven up the place."

"What's a covid rave?" Ed asked.

"It's a load of people getting together for a huge party, AND it's illegal," Tess told him.

"It couldn't come at a worse time," Fred continued. "One of my mates in the police told me to keep my eyes open because the emergency services are especially stretched. Loads of police are either on holiday or off sick with covid! It couldn't be a worse time. Also, the local hospitals are scared about the super spreader risk of the virus if there is a big gathering."

Plates of sizzling fish and chips had just arrived when they heard a police siren. "Maybe there's trouble on the beach, like you said." Ed dunked a chip in ketchup and watched the police car race by - blue lights flashing. "Perhaps there *is* a rave?"

By the Chippy on the Beach, it remained peaceful with small groups of locals enjoying their day. The friends munched and chatted. Suddenly they spotted an agitated Turdly speeding towards them – flapping and screeching to attract their attention. She came to a sudden halt in the sky and started twitching her beak towards Greatstone beach. As the friends stood up, they could see a mass of people on the sands.

"I'm sure I can hear music from here!" Lizzy frowned.

"This is just what I was talking about," Ivan said to the group, "And Turdly knows there's something wrong too. Look at her jumping about!"

"She wants us to follow her along the beach," Fred told them. "Sounds like trouble. We had better go and see if the police need a hand before this gets out of control."

"Come on!" Tess stuffed the last of her fish in her mouth. "You get in the car and park up as close as you can, we'll go ahead on our bikes and phone some of our mates for help. Let's do a nice charge along the seafront!"

"You'll take us, won't you?" Ed panicked. He imaged being stuck with the girls while the adults got stuck into an adventure.

"Of course!" Fred grinned. "This is serious stuff though."

Maggie and Lizzy flicked their long hair and applied lip gloss. Ed rolled his eyes and raced to the car, ensuring he got to sit in the front with Fred.

Soon they were at the scene and saw the two police officers – who they secretly called Little and Large – with the community warden. They were trying to reason with a crowd of more than two hundred. Music was blaring, there were crates of beer and a huge barbecue had been lit. The party people were settling in for a long rave, and although the group was peaceful, they would not be moved. Help was needed FAST…

"We need a bit of fun around here," Lizzy said to Maggie. "This day is turning out better than we expected!"

Unfortunately, her foolish comment was heard by the community warden, who swung around and spoke to her, "It might look like fun to you – but no one is going to be laughing if they get this virus. Stay and help us or go home."

"I'll help," Lizzy muttered, a blush spreading over her face. Maggie smiled and linked her arm in Lizzy's, showing her support for her friend.

Little and Large were trying to reason with the big group. PC Large, short and wiry, began, "Look every-one. We know you want to have a good time after being cooped-up for months, and we don't want to be spoil sports. But you are breaking the covid laws about social

"We don't want to be spoil sports, but you are breaking the covid laws about social distancing. What you are doing is illegal."

distancing. What you are doing is illegal. I know it's just started, and everyone is behaving themselves at the moment, but we cannot let you continue."

"It is a danger to yourselves and other people on the beach." PC Little, tall and stern, continued. "You need to break it up, or we'll have to. That will mean arrests and big fines for whoever started this."

The group leaders looked sullen. One shrugged his shoulders, took a swig of beer, and spoke, "We just want to have a good time, have a barbecue, play some music. Is that a crime?"

PC Little replied, "I am afraid it is! We don't want to spoil your fun, but you must keep to the law. Please split up into small groups of six, tone down the music, keep the barbecues small and do not get drunk."

"Keep your distance from other beach visitors," Large advised. "There is plenty of room on the beach for everyone. Come on, let's work together?"

The leaders turned their backs, and one gave a thumbs up to the man who had just set up loudspeakers. Music began to blare out and the ravers cheered.

The two policemen looked at each other in despair. Just then help arrived! There came the roar of motorbikes – Tess, Ivan and the New Romney Bikers. The police trudged across the sand and through the dunes to meet them in the carpark.

"Glad to see you all!" PC Little gave a huge grin. "Just in the nick of time! They have decided to ignore our friendly advice and carry on with this illegal party. There must be 200 people!"

"Can you help us distance everyone?" PC Large asked.

Ivan organised everyone into groups of two or three and asked them to go around and try to reason with the ravers. "Ask then to split up into smaller groups," he suggested. "Explain the rules and the risks. Tell them there is going to be fines if more police turn up. Main thing is to keep everything friendly and relaxed. Avoid any trouble."

Tess and Fred went to have a quiet word with the guys who had set up the temporary disco. It was so loud that the sand was shuddering as they stood and tried to make themselves heard. "Come on guys, let's move the kit down the beach. Keep it away from these families who have come for a quiet day with their children. And can you turn it down a bit. Look – the kids are scared." Gradually they got the situation under control.

The team went along the beach talking to everyone and giving them strong bags to put their rubbish in. All the team pushed the message, "If you bring food, drink and other stuff then take your rubbish home. If you litter the beach, it destroys the environment."

Before long, police reinforcements arrived. They were impressed with how everyone was now spread out, and the music was not too loud. Of course, not everyone was prepared to follow the rules, and a few arrests were made, but most of the ravers were friendly and behaved themselves. By early evening they had left Greatstone Beach.

The police inspector waved to the local bikers and the six friends, wanting them to come and see him. "Well done everyone! You have saved the day. In the end everyone had a nice time and there was no trouble. Good job!" Then he looked up to the sky and said, "But I've got to ask – what is that crazy bird? I've never seen anything like it!"

Turdly, who seemed to know what everyone said, did a loop-the-loop, followed by a pirouette! Everyone laughed!

Author's note: I remember there was an incident like this during lockdown, which required a significant police intervention to keep people safe from Covid. Over the years there have been reports of punch-ups on the Romney Marsh beaches between rival gangs. Nearby there were well-known battles between the Mods and Rockers on bank holidays in places like Hastings .

Beach Rescue

Turdly was cruising on a summer's day
Over the crowded beach,
Lots of people in the water
Blissfully unaware...
Turdly could see the danger
The wind had just shifted
The tide had turned
And was now blowing offshore
Sending all the flimsy inflatables
Rapidly out to sea.
Children screaming, parents panicking,
A major incident in the making...

Lilos... inflatable ducks... swans... even flamingos! One of the worst scenarios for the coastguards and lifeboat crews is a very crowded beach with a strong wind gusting off the shore. If the tide is going out, and people are playing about on these toys, then there is likely to be trouble. The offshore wind blows the different craft out to sea very quickly. With inexperienced kayakers and kite surfers as well, you soon have a major incident developing quickly with multiple small emergencies happening all along the beach.

Some beaches are patrolled by lifeguards, but many

are not. It can be the public who must alert the emergency services who then spring into action.

This is exactly what happened on a sunny, but breezy, early September day. There were still a lot of families on the beach enjoying their last days of holidays.

At St Mary's Bay, a group of Sea Cadets had come for a final outing with their three instructors before school holidays ended. The instructors had taught them a lot over the summer, and they wanted to practice their drills. The cadets were full of enthusiasm.

"Listen up everyone!" the chief instructor bellowed. "We are going to spilt into three groups. Group one will practice on the paddle boards and surfboards. Group two will practise beach rescue techniques. Group three will practise running on the beach and keep an eye on the other groups in case they get into difficulties."

The cadets called, "Aye, Aye, sir!"

On the beach, the visitors gathered, and by the seawall the car park filled up. The kiosks were opening, and people began to queue for drinks and ice-creams. With the sun shining, everyone had a smile on their face. They were going to appreciate the day.

While lots of people were digging in the golden sands, or paddling in the shallows, others were already floating about on their inflatable toys.

Some of the visitors spotted an unusual bird in the sky. Far larger than a seagull, with a long body, and black feathers tipped in red, orange and yellow, it was Turdly flying her usual beach patrol. "Eyes in the sky!" her friends would have said.

No one was expecting the wind to change, but change it did... And quickly! Just as the tide turned and began going out, the wind turned too. Turdly felt the rustle in her feathers, and she knew she must look out for trouble in the sea.

The exotic bird flew closer to the shore. Suddenly, there was panic amongst the parents on the beach. Turdly saw them running about shouting. She heard the fear in their voices. Several inflatables, with children riding on them, were being swept out to sea at the same time. This was seriously scary.

Turdly immediately flew over to where Ivan and Tess were sitting in Ivan's back garden enjoying a late breakfast. With her usual pattern of squawks and nodding of her head, they soon understood that help was needed.

"Come on Tess," Ivan said. "Looks like Turdly wants us to go towards St Mary's Bay. There's trouble there..."

Before they had put down their mugs of tea, Turdly was

gone and racing in the direction of Reed Farm.

Fred had already been working for hours and was now enjoying a brunch. Mrs Gaffer had just brought out bacon and egg rolls, and he ate them while sitting on a patch of grass, with his back against an old stone wall.

Just as he allowed his eyes to close and his body relaxed in the sunshine, he heard Maggie call out, "There's Turdly! Over there…"

The young farmhand sat up a little to watch the bird swoop down, and again she began a series of nods and screeches.

"Looks like we are needed at the coast," he muttered to himself. "I'll follow the byways and go on the quad bike. Best let Mrs Gaffer know…" He pulled himself to his feet and ran towards the farmhouse.

Minutes later, Fred was heading down a farm track on the quad. The phone was set up on hands-free and he was shouting to Ivan as he bounced over ruts and negotiated the turns. "Hiya mate! The bird is carrying on over something. Have you heard about any trouble at St Mary's Bay?" He listened to Ivan's response and answered, "I'll see you there," before ending the call. By the time Fred arrived on the beach, both the Dungeness and Littlestone lifeboats were approaching. There was a

A quad bike!" the coastguard exclaimed.
"I really need you!"

coastguards' car parked on the seawall.

"A quad bike!" the coastguard exclaimed. "I really need you!" He passed a megaphone. "Can you to alert us to where there is the greatest risk to lives. Your mates are already telling people to get out of the water. Some of these families can see it is dangerous, but they are still letting their kids go in the sea."

Fred could see Tess and Ivan speaking to beach-goers nearby, but the sands at St Mary's Bay stretched for miles to Dymchurch in the east and Greatstone in the west. It was a lot to cover.

As he spoke, they looked upwards. The familiar sound of the search and rescue helicopter could be heard. Then it came into sight, flying low over the sea. Already someone was at the hatch, ready to be lowered towards the water.

"I'll go towards Dymchurch," Fred suggested as he pointed the quad towards the popular holiday village. Adrenaline pumped through him as he began to warn families of the dangers. The water may be shallow, but it was no place for inflatable toys.

"Out of the water... We need to help the lifeboats and coastguards... It's not safe," he bellowed over and over.

At Dymchurch he met a coastguard who confirmed that

everything was now under control. "Thanks a lot," he said. "You've been a great help. It's all fine at this end, but if you could work your way back reminding people to keep out of the sea, I'd appreciate it."

"No problem," Fred replied. There was something good about being a small part of a team who were pulling together to help. As he returned to St Mary's Bay, he smiled to see that even the local sea cadets were playing their part.

Soon, the combined efforts made sure everyone was rescued, with a few minor injuries but no fatalities. More than twenty people were saved that day! A great result!

*

The next Monday evening, Fred arrived at a hall in St Mary's Bay. He gave a shy grin to the cadet instructor who greeted him at the door.

"Good to have you join us," the instructor said. "We could do with more volunteers like you on our team. I have a feeling that you'll be a real asset!"

Author's note – This draws on the major incident involving a multiple agency rescue operation in the summer of 2019 when a number of people were drowned on Camber Sands.

Snowed-Up and Iced-In

Turdly did not like the cold
Iced up feathers are no good
Tucked up warmly in the barn
Dozing happily… when Little Ed
Disturbs her reverie saying
Gaffer wants her to fly
Over to Old Sid/Lil's place
Because they are in trouble
Their phone has gone dead
After the first emergency call

In a tiny cottage with three rooms all in a row, and a roof made from thatch cut from the reeds lining nearby ditches, there lived an old couple called Sid and Lil. He had been a looker on the farm all his life – at least since he had been old enough to work the dogs and help with the lambing.

Looker is a Romney Marsh name for shepherd. 'I go looking here and looking there, making sure the sheep are safe' Sid would tell anyone who happened to ask. He had left school at twelve-years-old and never been off the marsh, other than to go to market at Rye or Ashford.

It was wintertime. Christmas had passed and those living on the farm faced the harshest months of the year. Gaffer had to make sure the sheep were safe, so they brought them to the fields closest to the farmyard. In the home, Mrs Gaffer made sure the larder was full of food, just in case they got snowed in. Fred worked long hours in the small areas of woodland, pulling out dead branches and cutting them up for the fire. The children left home for the school bus while it was still dark and returned after sunset. They all had to think of Sid and Lil in their lonely cottage and make sure they were warm, dry and well-fed.

One afternoon in February, the sky turned an odd shade of purple-grey and before long the snow began to fall thick and fast.

"We've done all we can to keep the animals safe, so that's our work finished for the day," the Gaffer announced. But the work on a farm was never done and they all knew that Gaffer would be checking on the animals whenever he felt the need to.

The family retreated to the warmth of the farmhouse kitchen, while Fred went to his small flat above the garage. Every so often one of them would pull back the curtains and look out to see the snowflakes drifting down, and soon they were carpeting the farmhouse garden, the stone walls and the yard.

After a couple of hours there was a rapping on the door and Fred came in. "My electricity has gone out. Look! The wires have broken." His voice was rushed, and he nodded in the direction of the cable running to his home. "Can I come in?"

"Make yourself comfy by the fire," Mrs Gaffer welcomed him. "Now where are those candles?" As she pulled a box of candles and matches out from under the kitchen sink, their lights began to flicker, and the television turned itself off. By the time she had set out candles on saucers, the farmhouse had lost its power too.

"At least we can keep warm in here. I'm glad we didn't bother with central heating," Gaffer announced. "You know where you are with a nice log burner. We can keep ourselves cosy and there's a dinner cooking on the top."

By the next morning, the snow was reaching the windowsills of the old farmhouse.

"It's stopped for now," Fred observed. "I reckon we should start on digging paths across the yard." He

looked up at the sky. "There's more snow due."

Ed stood beside him at the window. "No school today!" He grinned and raced upstairs to tell Maggie.

"You're right about the snow." Gaffer joined them at the window. "It's not over yet." The sky looked ready to empty its load over Reed Farm and the surrounding land. Then on the roof of the barn, at the entrance to her shelter, he spotted a forlorn looking creature. Turdly, usually so lively, was sitting with her long neck bent, head tucked into her chest, and shoulders hunched. "Turdly doesn't like this weather," he said.

"You're right," Fred agreed. "Who knows where she came from. I've never seen a bird like her, but I bet she's from some place where it's always sunny. There's a splendid home up there, but she looks cold. We should persuade her to go inside where we put plenty of hay to keep her snug."

"Maybe she knows that snow brings problems, and she has to keep a watch out," Mrs Gaffer suggested. "I'll find some tasty seeds to cheer her up. Or maybe a bit of stale cake?"

The next hour passed with the men busy at work in the yard. Every so often, Turdly would fly in a circle around the farm, but without her usual excitable squawks and loop-the-loops.

When the snow began to fall again, the front door opened and Mrs Gaffer called out, "Sid has phoned. It's Lil – she's really ill and he's worried sick."

"I'll phone him back," the Gaffer replied. "I wanted to check on him anyway."

"You can't!" Mrs Gaffer wailed. "His battery died on that old mobile, and the landline isn't working. They are stuck out there with no power and Lil has got a temperature. She's burning up, he says!"

As they spoke, it seemed as if Turdly knew there was trouble. She sprang into life, darting off in the direction of the old cottage where Sid and Lil lived. Gaffer and Mrs Gaffer watched her go. "I don't know how I'm going to reach them through this snow," the Gaffer said, "but I have a feeling that Turdly will let us know if they are in trouble."

They took it in turns to look out for the strange bird and after ten minutes Turdly could be seen battling through the thick snowflakes. She swooped low, dropping a rolled-up piece of paper, then retreated to her shelter on the barn roof. Ed picked it up and showed the others. "Look at this!"

"'Help! Lil very ill. Struggling to breathe. Snowed in.'"

Mrs Gaffer read. "We had better call 999. There's no point in trying the doctor – he won't be able to reach the cottage." She was already picking up her mobile phone and within seconds the call had been answered. "Ambulance please," Mrs Gaffer said. She explained their worries about Lil.

The others listened in and waited for Mrs Gaffer to tell them about the call. "They can't send an ambulance. It would never get along these country lanes, and it's dangerous to fly a helicopter."

"We need to clear the track to the cottage," the Gaffer responded, already pulling on his wellies. "I don't know if it will be any use, but we can't just sit about here and do nothing. I'll get the snow plough on the tractor."

With Fred wielding the shovel and Gaffer on the tractor, it took nearly two hours for them to reach Sid and Lil's cottage. By then the snow had stopped falling and Turdly was hovering nervously. When they managed to open the front door, Gaffer and Fred found Lil bundled up in blankets on the settee, her face red and breathing slow. She barely looked at them and made no attempt to rise from where she lay.

"I'm so worried," Sid told them. "Her chest is rattling, and she is coughing something terrible. She won't eat

Turdly was hovering nervously

or even talk to me. That's not like Lil, is it?"

"It's stopped snowing," Gaffer replied. "There's no time to waste. I'll call for an air ambulance from my mobile, and Fred can start shifting snow, so it has somewhere to land."

Before the words had left his mouth, Gaffer could see Fred running to the tractor. At that moment, Turdly shot up high into the sky, performed a pirouette and flew off at top speed. Gaffer made the call and spent several minutes discussing the situation, all the time trying to hide his concern from Sid and Lil. With a heavy heart, he turned to Sid when the called ended, "They can't send an air ambulance. There isn't one free."

"What's that then?" Sid asked, as he looked out of the window.

Gaffer frowned. The sound of a beating engine boomed in the grey sky and a headlight shone, giving hope to those watching it approach. Colours formed around the light – red and white – then the spinning blades took shape. Mesmerised, they watched as it headed directly towards them.

"The coastguards' search and rescue helicopter!" Gaffer murmured, stunned to see it now almost above them. "It's a bit off course!" He moved outside to feel the vibrations running through his body. Now the air was filled with the noise from what looked like a gigantic mechanical insect. If that wasn't exhilarating enough for those on the ground – there behind it was Turdly. A mere speck in the sky, but definitely the crazy bird who was now a huge part of their lives.

"Looks like Lil's going to get a joy ride to hospital!" Gaffer yelled at Sid who stood in the open doorway of the cottage.

With bated breath, they watched as Lil was checked over by the crew, then carefully cocooned in thick blankets before being lifted onto a stretcher. The old lady managed to raise her hand before the doors were closed and the helicopter prepared to rise into the sky.

They watched until the headlight faded into the merest speck in the sky, then Gaffer said to Sid, "This is no good for any of us standing about in the cold. Mrs Gaffer won't be happy if we leave you here on your own." Sid returned to the farmhouse and waited for news of Lil while the sun set and the whole area was bathed in that eerie light you find when darkness falls on a snowy land.

It was early evening when the phone rang, and Mrs Gaffer spoke to a nurse from the hospital in Ashford.

"That's wonderful news," they heard her say. "Yes, we'll look after Sid. There's no need for Lil to worry." When she put the phone down, Mrs Gaffer reported, "They've given Lil some medicine and she's much better already. Isn't that good news?"

Sighs of relief travelled around those gathered in the farmhouse kitchen

"It's all thanks to Turdly again!" Ed laughed. "It was a lucky day for Lil when that crazy bird arrived."

"It was a lucky day for all of us," Fred added.

"The nurse said that your son and his wife have been able to reach the hospital," Mrs Gaffer told Sid. "She's not on her own."

"Well! There's a tale to tell the grandchildren," Old Sid grinned. "The day when Granny-Lil was saved by a bird! Now, did you say there was some apple pie? I'd lost my appetite, but it seems to have returned!"

Author's note: – Again this draws on my personal memories of a story like this being recounted to me by a farmer friend on the Marsh.

Beach Landings

The sad tale story of the many groups of refugees currently landing on the shores of Romney Marsh

Turdly was patrolling the shore
On a clear very early morning
Just as the sun was dawning
Her eyes in the sky saw the rib landing
People scrambling quickly up the shingle
Just east of the lifeboat station…

Very early one May morning, when the sea was flat calm, and the sky took on the pinkish hue of pre-dawn, a large inflatable rib landed on the beach at Greatstone. A bedraggled group of three families, including women and children, clambered out.

Their leader, Karim, preceded them as they paddled through shallow water to the dry sand. When they reached the shingle bank, he leaned down, gathering a pile of stones and lifting them to his lips to kiss. "God is merciful! He has brought us safely to England at last. Quick, brothers and sisters, let us leave this boat and our troubles behind us. I know you are cold and weary, but we must move fast. This place is too quiet, and we will be easily spotted once the sun rises."

His brother Abdul responded, "I have the map we were given. It shows the way to the railway station. First, we walk along the beach, and when we reach the lighthouse, we move inland. It is not far. From there we will see the station buildings."

As the sun began to peep over the horizon, they trailed along the beach towards Dungeness. Each one of them carried a small bag. These held their only belongings – their only links with past lives. There were few people on the beach at that time, and it seemed as if the new arrivals had not been noticed.

Before long, Amira, one of the women, said. "We are all

so tired, and the children need to eat. Can we rest?"

"Will there be food?" her sister-by-marriage Leila asked.

Abdul showed them a map and pointed to the railway station. "It is not far. The good man who helped us get here has said we must ask for the first train to London. The station will be busy, and no one will notice us. I have money to buy food."

The women were satisfied and told the children. "We can feed you soon. Today you will eat English food!" The children gazed back with their huge dark eyes. They were too scared and too tired to smile.

"When we get to the station we can rest and eat before we catch the train to London," Karim added. "Once we get to London, we can contact our relatives and God willing we will be safe!"

Iqubal, who was the head of the third family group, suggested, "Those of us who are stronger must help those who are weaker. But let us make haste before it gets lighter. We must reach the station before the sun has fully risen."

The people traffickers who had been paid to help these families reach England had not told them that the railway station was for a miniature railway. There was no train to London. This was the Romney, Hythe and

Dymchurch Railway, and the furthest they could travel to was Hythe. The café did serve delicious meals, but it would not be open for hours. The asylum seekers had been tricked. As the sun rose over Dungeness, they would soon attract attention.

Assistance was urgently needed!

While the group trudged along the shingle, making their way towards the station, Turdly was having an early morning patrol. She spotted the group and knew something was wrong. These were not fishermen or bird-watchers or litter-pickers. It was very odd.

It was not early for Fred who was working on Reed Farm fixing some fencing. He liked to get up at dawn and start work. As he reached for the mallet, a movement in the sky caused him to pause. Fred frowned and squinted as he looked towards the sun, then murmured, "I'm sure it's that bird again!"

Turdly flapped in, squawking excitedly, and nodding her head towards Dungeness. The feathers on the crest of her head quivered madly. Fred shook his head in wonder. "I don't know what to make of her, but it looks like help is needed."

The quad bike was to hand, so he jumped on it, as always taking the farm tracks to find a more direct route to the coast.

He arrived to find the exhausted group squatting on the ground outside the station building. Children were crying, and the men were looking about the place.

"We are waiting for the train to London," Karim explained in broken English. He looked across at the narrow tracks, built to pull a tourist train. "I think we have been tricked."

"You've come here by boat, haven't you?" Fred asked. It was obvious these people were not day trippers.

"We have just arrived on the beach," Karim admitted. "We were told by the people trafficker that we could take the train from here to London. Our relatives are expecting us! We will be safe!"

Abdul and Iqubal stood beside their brother. The others cowered on the ground, gazing up at this man who they hoped would help them.

"I don't know much about that kind of thing," Fred admitted. "I work on a farm. But I'll try… I'll try to help. Just let me have a think."

Why had he followed Turdly? Why had she asked him to help when all he knew about was fixing things and working on the land? Fred felt a blind panic envelope him. This wasn't the sort of thing he was any good at. He faltered, all sorts of things rushing through his mind and none of them any use to these tired, hungry people.

Fred realised that the station master had pulled up in his car, and the arrivals had all turned to watch him approach. He gave a nod to Fred. "It looks like we have visitors," he said. "What's going on? Are you dealing with it?" A huge bunch of keys rattled in his hand. "It's a bit early for a train ride."

"They've come in by boat," Fred confirmed. "But no, I'm not dealing with it. I want to help, but I don't know how. Look at them – it doesn't matter where they have come from, or why they are here. We must help them."

"I can see that," the station master responded. "But I've got my work to get on with. Are the police on their way? They'll sort it out."

"Police?" Fred repeated. "I don't know. But look at them – these people need our support. Can you imagine what they have been through to get here, because I can't." He felt himself getting angry with the station master. Surely he wasn't going to ignore these desperate people? "Can we take them into the station?" he asked. "We need to give them warm food, blankets, dry clothes, and hot water to wash with."

"I can start on food," the station master replied, finding the key to the main door. "But the police need to be told." He pulled his mobile phone from his pocket and started dialling 999.

"Thank you!" Fred felt himself relax a little.

By this time, some of the locals had seen what was happening. A few of them approached Fred with blankets. "Here you go," a woman said. "It's not much but they will be cold."

When did I become in charge? Fred wondered, but he took the blankets and murmured his thanks while ushering the bedraggled group into the station building.

When the station master had finished on the phone, he said, "The police have asked that we keep them safe here. Border force have been alerted, and police officers are on their way. In the meantime, let's hear what they have to say…"

While they sipped at hot chocolate and munched on

toast, the men and women told their story.

The group was made up of three families from Syria, who had fled from terrible troubles to nearby Turkey. There were three sets of parents and children, one grandfather and one grandmother, and two uncles.

While at the camp in Turkey they had made their applications for asylum in the UK. The adults were educated, and it seemed as if they would be allowed to travel to England. However, huge delays from the UK side made them impatient. Then a family member became sick and needed urgent medical treatment. The men decided that they had no choice but to arrange travel themselves through people traffickers. It cost them all their money and meant they would be entering the country illegally.

They hoped that if they made it to the UK, the immigration authorities would treat them kindly. After many difficult weeks, they reached Calais, from where they made their crossing on the third attempt.

All the locals who heard the story took this brave and humble group to their hearts. They vowed to do what they could to help. When Border Force arrived, they spoke first to the local police. Then they allowed Fred to tell the story of how the families came to be there.

Overwhelmed by this responsibility, he did his best.

"Thank you, my friend," Karim said when Fred had finished.

"I hope it was good enough," Fred replied. He knew nothing about these people and how they had suffered. It was time to learn more, he vowed.

The officials needed to understand these were genuine refugees seeking political asylum, and it seemed they were sympathetic. Border Force then took the families away to a centre but asked if Ed and Fred would be prepared to support their case, and if the locals would speak up for them. They all agreed.

After several months, there came some wonderful news. The asylum application was granted and the group of families who landed at Dungeness on that May morning were given permission to live in the UK.

A happy ending!

Authors note: Refuges seeking asylum and safety landing on the beach in a desperate state are a sad reality on the Marsh coast between Folkestone and Pett Level where I live. They are increasing all the time, desperate and abused by ruthless people traffickers.

There was a major rescue carried out by the Eastbourne RNLI in October where the crew and asylum seekers were abused by members of the public on landing. There was a similar incident in Hastings. Local groups and volunteers have responded magnificently to support these groups of refugees when they first land on the beach.

These arrivals can cause tensions between the rescue services (RNLI/Coastguard/Border Force/Police etc), who are just performing their humanitarian duties, and some uninformed sections of the general public.

Unfortunately, many refugees seeking asylum and safety do not fully appreciate the real situation in the UK, what sort of reception they will receive and the delays it can take to process applications. Because they have not gone through the official channels they will be considered as illegal. Admittedly one of the main issues is that access to official channels outside the UK are very limited and the processes very slow. The web and social media often paint a much rosier picture than the reality. There is a major role for social media to show a truer and clearer picture of the actual conditions which refugees will face on arrival. It is important to understand that according to United Nations Refugee Agency definition there is a clear distinction between being a refugee who is seeking political asylum to escape war, conflict, persecution which threaten their families lives and those who are choosing to leave their countries to seek asylum in the UK for economic reasons in order to improve their family's lives .

The story and characters are fictitious but based on the truth.

Since writing this story the number of refugees crossing the channel have increased exponentially this autumn (September/October/November 2021), with multiple landings at Dungeness/Pett Level/Hastings.

Tess and Ivan's Wedding

Turdly thought Tess was great,
Feisty, independent and quirky
She felt they were kindred spirits
Because she was a bit like her...

"I'll marry you when my tattoo has gone!" Tess laughed at Ivan. "I've told you that!"

Ivan had come knocking at Tess's door at 5am that morning, with a flask of hot chocolate, and a silly grin on his face. Now they were sitting on the seafront at Littlestone watching the sun rise. As the glowing ball peeped over the horizon, the sky to the east became rich with streaks of orange and yellow. It was a show like no other and one that changed every day. Yet by the time the hot chocolate had been drained from chunky mugs, the colours were fading to more subtle shades and the whole sky had changed from rich navy to a pale grey-blue.

The day was going to be scorching hot, but in the early morning there was still a chill in the air, so Tess wore a cardigan over her summer dress.

"I know you did!" Ivan grinned. "Will you marry me?" He pulled back the cardigan to show the tattoo had vanished.

"How?" Tess frowned. She loved the colourful picture of a dragon which had been created in Bangkok two years before. It wasn't a permanent tattoo, but she hoped it would stay a bit longer. She would have wanted it to remain forever, if the name of a former love was not displayed across the arch of the dragon's back. 'Charlie' it said, in elaborate swirls.

"I liked it too – apart from the name," Ivan admitted. "But I love you more! Will you marry me?"

"Of course!" Tess was still looking on her arm. "I'll marry you, but I can't help wondering why it vanished so quickly."

At that moment, there was the rumble of a tractor approaching. You don't often see a great beast like that on the seafront, but Ed and Fred wanted to arrive in style! Ed was carrying a bunch of flowers and Fred had a basket with warm croissants and strawberries.

"Congratulations!!" they called.

"How did they know?" Tess asked, but she couldn't help

laughing. They were going to get married, and their best friends were there to share the good news. But where was that tattoo? Ivan had a funny little smile. She scowled at him.

"OK..." he began. "You told me it wasn't permanent but it didn't seem to be going anywhere. You know that body lotion I bought you?"

"Yes," Tess replied. She was beginning to work it out.

"It had ink remover cream in it." He tried to keep a straight face, but Ivan couldn't stop himself from roaring with laughter. The others joined in, and even Tess began to see the funny side of it. It looked like being married to Ivan was going to be entertaining!

*

Tess & Ivan got married
At their church on the Romney Marsh.
With all their friends around them
It was a very joyful affair.

No one was surprised to find out that Tess and Ivan's wedding was a bit daft! Everyone thought Ivan would arrive on his motorbike – instead he came trundling along the lane in the Gaffer's biggest tractor with his best man, Fred, alongside him. They wore smart suits –

with bright pink socks showing, just for fun!

The church was ancient and small. It squatted not far from Reed Farm, in the Romney Marsh countryside, surrounded by sheep fields and waterways. The path to it was no more than an earth track, used by sheep more than humans, and the tower supported three bells which rang out across the desolate land.

Tess had ordered the men to wear something pink! The socks matched her bright hair and the flowers sewn onto the neckline and hem of her long, flowing dress. The bridesmaids – and there were a lot of them – included Aeleen and Charleen from the pub at Dungeness, as well as Maggie and Lizzy. Between them they carried a huge, gilded cage and in it was – yes, you guessed it – Turdly Turd the Exotic Bird! How they got the bird in a cage, nobody knew. She didn't seem to mind though!

At the end of the ceremony, the vicar suggested it was time to kiss the bride. However, Tess and Ivan grinned at each other, then rolled up their sleeves to show everyone their new matching tattoos!

When they left the church, the bikers in their leathers were lined up outside. There was a great cheer, and they led the way to the coast. Tess and Ivan scrambled up into the tractor and followed at a slower pace.

At the Chippy on the Beach, there was work to be done! Bridesmaids, Aeleen and Charleen, had to spring into action – it was fish and chips all round for the guests. While Tess and Ivan kept busy talking to their friends and family, people sat on benches outside or sprawled on rugs on the ground. The Bikers Band kept the live music flowing, and the old fishermen entertained a group of people who were ready to believe their tall tales. Nearby, the sea rolled up the beach to crash on the shingle bank, and the gulls screamed to each other as they swooped in the sky.

"What a day!" Fred smiled. "Music, good food and the sea... Plus, our best mates have got married."

"Where's Turdly?" Ed asked. He was sitting on a thick rug with Fred, Maggie and Lizzy. They had just finished eating. The girls, both bridesmaids, were looking pretty in long pink dresses and flowers in their hair. Ed couldn't help thinking that Lizzy looked more than pretty – beautiful! He scowled – an elegant dress and delicate make-up couldn't stop the girls from being annoying most of the time!

"Turdly?" Fred repeated, feeling lazy after eating. It was good to have a day off. Later he would ask Aeleen to dance with him, or perhaps go for a romantic walk. He eyed the expanse of stones – he might have to put an arm around her to keep her steady. Fred's thoughts returned to Ed's question about the bird. "She's up on the roof, watching us."

They gazed upwards. Turdly was nestled by the chimney. She appeared to be dozing, but one eye was busy scanning the area.

"That's OK then," Ed replied. "I was thinking she had gone a bit quiet." He wondered if Lizzy would like an ice cream, and would she laugh if he offered to get her one.

Their thoughts were disturbed by Aeleen coming over and flopping down on the rug. "Have you heard?" she asked, as everyone made space for her.

"Heard what?" Maggie wondered.

"It's the honeymoon!" Aeleen wailed. "It's not fair. Tess and Ivan are the type of people who help everyone, and it's not right that it has all gone wrong for them."

"What's gone wrong?" Everyone was sitting up now. Even Turdly had her neck craned towards them.

"It's cancelled. The hotel has been closed," Aeleen explained. "They can't just turn up at the airport and fly off when there's nowhere to stay."

At that moment, Turdly stretched her body out to its full height. She ruffled her feathers and pushed herself up, standing on her tippy-toes. Then the quirky bird flew off, as straight as an arrow, in the direction of Lydd.

Sadly, the friends didn't notice the bird leave her spot on the roof of the Pilot. If they had seen her, then they would have known not to worry.

*

Within twenty minutes, a red sports car was racing along the road to Dungeness. It stopped, scattering stones, causing everyone to turn towards it. A tall, slim man in a smart suit leapt out and ran (the best he could on the stony ground) towards Fred and Ed.

"You know the bird – Turdly, is it?" he asked. "She's causing mayhem at the airport. And I don't know how, but I have a feeling she wants me to come here and talk to you."

"Of course, she does!" Fred yelled with joy, taking his chance to put an arm around Aeleen who had agreed to a walk later.

"It's not every day a bird tells me what to do, and I'm feeling a bit silly," the airport manager admitted. "What's going on?"

"Tess and Ivan have had their honeymoon cancelled,"

Ed explained. It had taken a moment for him to catch up, but now it all made sense.

"And you have an airport," Maggie continued. "With planes…"

"To take people on holiday," Lizzy added.

"Can you help?" Fred asked. "Can they have their holiday?"

"Bring them along to Ferryfield in an hour!" the manager said. "I'll find a way to take them away somewhere decent!"

*

With the bikers leading the way, Tess and Ivan were once more in the tractor with Fred driving.

"I can't believe we are going on holiday!" Tess shouted above the roar of the engine.

"And no long drive to one of the big airports!" Ivan yelled.

"It's all thanks to Turdly!" Fred bellowed.

Soon they were all parking up at the airport. The bikers in black leather lined up, then there was the huge tractor, and numerous cars belonging to wedding guests.

The airport manager was waiting to greet them at the entrance. "Have you got your passports ready?" he asked. "And suitcases packed for a week in the sun?"

"We have!" Tess and Ivan chorused.

"This plane..." he nodded towards a silver aeroplane turning on the runway. "This plane is taking you to Pisa in Italy! It's a new flight we are about to start running from here. We were going to do a practice run today, and a crazy bird told me you'd like to come along!"

Then off they went to Ferryfield,
Having enjoyed their wedding feast
Before their flight arrived
To fly them off to the east...

Turdly danced a special dance
As Tess was her special friend
And squawked a very special song
Until she left them at the gate.

Once the pair were airborn,
Their guests kicked their shoes off
And partied until dawn

Author's note: This is just a bit of fun to round off the tales with a happy ending!!